Little
Red Riding
Hood

STERLING CHILDREN'S BOOKS

New York

TEXT ADAPTATION GIADA FRANCIA

GRAPHIC DESIGN MARINELLA DEBERNARDI

FROM A FAIRY TALE BY THE
Brothers Grimm

ILLUSTRATIONS BY
Francesca Rossi

In a quiet country village there once lived a cheerful little girl. Everyone knew her for her smile, and for the red cape with a hood that she wore every day. We all have a name, and the little girl was no exception. But because she always wore her red cape, people in the village started to call her Little Red Riding Hood. Why did she like her red cape so much? Well, there was a very simple explanation.

One day after school, the girl came home to a wonderful surprise. Her grandmother, whom she loved dearly, had come to visit her for her birthday. Grandmother lived deep in the woods, so Little Red Riding Hood rarely saw her. On this occasion, however, she had come all the way to the village and brought with her two baskets. The first contained a home-baked cherry tart. It was shaped like a daisy, because her grandmother knew how much she liked to pick flowers. The second basket contained the best birthday gift she had ever received: a cape of her favorite color, which her grandmother had made especially for her.

After spending a few days together in the village, the grandmother had to return home. Little Red Riding Hood did not want her to leave, but the grandmother promised that she would come to visit her again at the village fair in summer. The little girl took to wearing her favorite cape every day.

When the day of the fair finally arrived, however, Little Red Riding Hood received some bad news.

"Your grandmother cannot come as she promised, my child," said her mother. "I'm afraid she is not feeling well, so she has to stay in bed for a few days."

"But who will cook for her?" asked the girl. "Who will help her?"

"I'll leave tomorrow when your father comes back from the market. I have prepared a basket of goods and—"

"Let me go! Please, Mother!" the girl begged. "I could stay with Grandmother for a few days and keep her company."

"I don't know," her mother replied uncertainly. "You would have to go through the woods and be very careful. . ."

"I'll be careful! I promise!"

"And you promise not to stop to talk to anyone? You promise to go straight to your grandmother's house without straying from the path?"

"Of course!" the girl replied earnestly.

Her mother gave in. "All right. Take this basket, and remember to stay on the path!"

"Don't worry, Mother, I'll do as you say," promised Little Red Riding Hood.

But as soon as she entered the woods, she forgot all her mother's advice. How beautiful the woods were in summer! The birds were singing and the squirrels jumped from tree to tree, making Little Red Riding Hood laugh. She wanted to follow them.

"I'll just go to the big oak tree over there and then come back onto the path that leads to Grandmother's." But when she reached the oak tree, she skipped over to a stream. And since she had gone that far, why shouldn't she just go and see what was around that bend?

In no time at all, Little Red Riding Hood found herself in the thick of the woods, home to the most feared animal in the forest: the big, bad wolf. The wolf heard the girl's laughter from afar and followed the merry sound.

"A little girl in the middle of the woods?" the wolf said to himself. "She must be lost. Nobody from the village ever comes here. Bad for her and good for me. She will make a superb lunch!"

"Hello, little one," asked the wolf as he trotted up to her. "What's your name? And what are you doing in this part of the forest?"

"Everyone calls me Little Red Riding Hood. I'm going to visit my grandmother, who is sick. She lives in the cottage under the three large oak trees. Are you the big, bad wolf that everybody talks about?"

"Me? A bad wolf? No! Not me! There must be some misunderstanding."

After considering what the girl had said, the wolf decided to make a meal of Little Red Riding Hood and her grandmother as well. But to make his plan work, the wolf had to get to the grandmother's cottage before the child. He could eat the old woman and then he would wait for the girl.

"What are you taking to your grandmother, little one?"

"A cake and some bread and cheese. Would you like a taste?"

"No, thank you," replied the wolf politely. He had a different banquet in mind. But first he had to delay the child long enough for him to be able to reach the grandmother first. "Don't you want to bring her some flowers, too?"

"I love flowers!" replied Little Red Riding Hood excitedly. "And I'd love to pick some for Grandmother. I'm sure that they will bring a smile to her face, even though she is ill."

The wolf smiled, and his long, sharp fangs glinted under his whiskers. "The ones I've seen nearby are unique, you know. They are brightly colored and they smell wonderful. Unfortunately, they don't bloom for very long. I'm sure tomorrow they will begin to fade. You should pick them today to fully enjoy their beauty."

"Oh, Wolf, please tell me where I can find them!"

"Go along this path, then turn right at the thorny hedge, then left at the waterfall, go past the ravine, and you're almost there," said the wolf, inventing the directions off the top of his head.

"Thank you, Wolf. You know, you're a lot nicer than people say! Some people in the village say that you're fierce and always hungry, but anyone can see you're not really like that. You didn't even want a piece of cheese! Don't worry. I'll tell everyone the truth," said Little Red Riding Hood. Then she set off in the direction the wolf had pointed out.

"Well done, little one. Go and get lost in the woods, while I run to your grandmother!" chuckled the wolf. He watched the child until she disappeared behind a large oak tree. As soon as he was sure she was not coming back, the wolf set off in the opposite direction.

The wolf followed the path through the forest that led to the grandmother's house under the three oak trees. As he walked, he congratulated himself on his excellent plan. It was a great day, but one that had started so terribly! That very morning, at dawn, a ray of sunlight had entered his den. It struck him in the face and woke him up with a jolt. The forest resounded with the songs of birds celebrating the glorious summer day, but when the wolf finally got up he was in a bad mood. He became even more moody when he heard the footsteps of that tedious hunter right outside his den.

For days, the wolf had been hunted by that man. He had managed to avoid the hunter, but it was becoming a real nuisance! Every time the hunter was in the forest, the wolf had to keep looking over his shoulder. One time the wolf was even forced to abandon the trail of a rabbit that he was hoping to have for dinner, and hide in the branches of a tree to avoid being seen.

It was not fair! The big, bad wolf was a great and ferocious hunter. Being seen hiding in a tree was not good for his reputation! Thinking about it now, he became angry all over again. He could still hear the laughter of the squirrels who had seen him hide.

The big, bad wolf increased his pace to make sure he would get to the grandmother's cottage first. He was just beginning to think that he had taken the wrong path when he finally saw the cottage amid the trees at the very edge of the forest. He had finally arrived and there was still no trace of Little Red Riding Hood. The wolf grinned: he would have time to carry out his plan.

Suddenly, he heard a noise. Fearing that it was the hunter, he quickly crouched down. But when he saw a mouse peeping out from the bushes he began to laugh.

"Go on, little one," he said generously. "Yesterday I would have grabbed you right away, but today I'm after much bigger prey!" Then he turned and knocked on the door of the cottage.

When she heard the unexpected knock, Little Red Riding Hood's grandmother sat up in bed. She wondered who could possibly be knocking on her door.

For a moment, she thought it must be that nuisance of a hunter again. For days, that irritating man had been wandering around in the woods near her cottage looking for a wolf. Several times he had come knocking at her door to ask if she had seen one. For this reason, there was irritation in her voice when she replied.

"Who is it?" she called without getting out of bed.

Outside the door, the wolf cleared his throat. Then, imitating the little girl, he said, "It's me, Little Red Riding Hood. Grandmother, I've brought you food and I've come to keep you company until you feel better."

The grandmother let out a sigh of relief. "Come in, my dear! The door's open."

She had barely finished speaking when the big, bad wolf burst into the cottage.

He swallowed the grandmother in one gulp and then lay down on the floor, satisfied.

"It's a long time since I've had such a good lunch," he said to himself. "And now it's the little girl's turn! Unfortunately she won't be able to tell anyone how kind the big, bad wolf is, because she won't be going back to the village!"

The wolf patted his stomach.

"And then, for dessert, I'll take home the basket with the cake. I could invite the weasel and the fox! They'd die of envy if they knew where I am now. Yes, celebrating with them is a great idea. I will tell them every detail of what happened today and then they'll have to admit that I am the most dangerous animal in the forest!"

Chuckling to himself, the wolf reflected on his lucky day. As he waited in the cottage, he thought about how best to surprise Little Red Riding Hood when she arrived. Then he came up with an idea:

"I'll disguise myself as Little Red Riding Hood's grandmother!"

The big, bad wolf dressed himself in the grandmother's nightgown, put on her spectacles, and settled down comfortably in her bed to wait for her granddaughter.

"The little girl must surely have realized by now that the flowers I told her about don't exist!" said the wolf, expecting her to arrive at any moment. After a few hours of waiting, however, he realized that he was wrong.

Little Red Riding Hood was small, but very determined. And above all, she was convinced that the rare and marvelous flowers that the wolf had spoken of would help her grandmother to get better. She had set out in the direction the wolf had indicated, and had soon reached the thorny hedge of which he had spoken. Among its branches, she had seen something. It was yellow, it was big, it was . . . a beehive!

As soon as Little Red Riding Hood touched the hive, a swarm of angry bees came after her, forcing her to hide among the reeds of a lake. The bees continued to buzz in a menacing tone over her head for a good hour until they finally drifted away.

Little Red Riding Hood came out of her hiding place and saw a waterfall at the end of the lake. Perhaps this was the one the wolf mentioned, the girl thought. She dried out in the sun and nibbled a slice of the cake in her basket. Then she got up, shook the crumbs off her cape, and continued on her way.

"The forest is so beautiful in summer!" she exclaimed, skipping along the narrow path. "I wonder why Mother gave me all those warnings. Even the big, bad wolf turned out to be very polite. I just can't understand what is so dangerous!"

As soon as she said this, Little Red Riding Hood almost fell into a deep ravine that cut straight through the forest. It was a terrifying chasm, but Little Red Riding Hood smiled. "See? There's even a bridge so that you can cross safely."

The bridge had actually been abandoned for some time and was nothing more than a few ropes and some rotting beams tied together with loose knots. But Little Red Riding Hood whistled as she skipped across it.

When she arrived on the other side of the ravine, she saw that it was a part of the forest where no one had been for years. Families of rabbits and squirrels were everywhere, and Little Red Riding Hood amused herself by chasing them.

"If I remember correctly, the wolf said that the field with the flowers is near the ravine. I just have to find a rare and colorful flower with which to surprise Grandmother," said the girl, looking around carefully. "There! Now that's an unusual flower! You don't often see one of those in the woods."

The girl walked over to a large oak tree. Between its roots a brightly colored plant had sprung up. It had a very strange shape. The petals seemed to open like a mouth. Little Red Riding Hood went over for a closer look at the flower. When she went to pick it, the petals closed over her fingers like teeth.

"Ouch! That hurt," cried the little girl, jumping back and sucking her thumb. "Ugh, I'm tired and sore. I'll count to ten, and then I'll stop. And never mind if I haven't found the flowers! One . . . two . . ."

When she got to ten, Little Red Riding Hood opened her eyes and gasped!

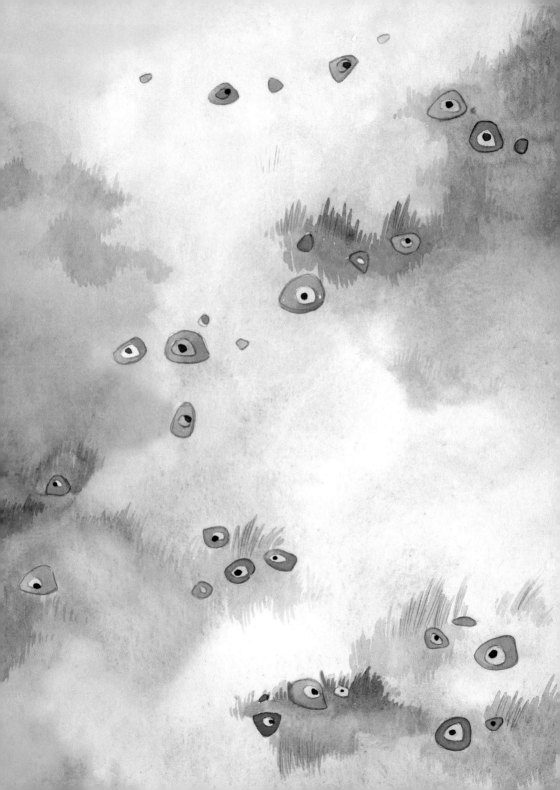

She had found them at last! They were fragrant and colorful, just as the wolf had described them. Little Red Riding Hood spent a long time carefully choosing which flowers to pick, until she was finally happy with the large bouquet that she had made. She placed it carefully in the basket and looked around, not sure which path led to her grandmother's house. She chose a small road that went downhill and started to follow it.

She had just taken the first steps when she saw the tip of a weapon sticking out from behind a rock!

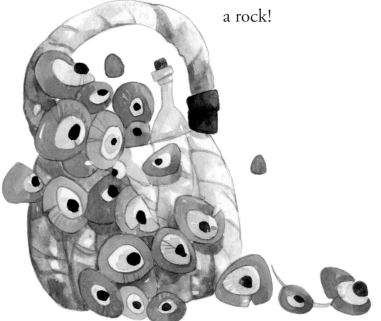

"Please don't hurt me!" she called out.

A big man with a bushy beard appeared from behind the rock, looking surprised. It was the hunter on the trail of the big, bad wolf. He had heard the cracking of twigs and had crept up, hoping to surprise the beast—but instead he found himself looking at a little girl!

"This hunt is becoming more difficult and tiring than I imagined," the hunter said softly.

On more than one occasion, it seemed that he had come very close to the wolf he had been tracking for days. Once he even thought he had seen the tip of a thick gray tail dangling from the branch of a tree—but when he looked again he could see only the squirrels, who seemed to be having fun watching him.

He shook his head and approached the girl.

"Who are you? What's your name?" he asked irritably.

"Well, everyone calls me Little Red Riding Hood because of the red cape that—"

"Okay, never mind. But tell me: where are you going, Little Red Riding Hood? Don't you know that this part of the forest is very dangerous?"

"I don't agree, sir. I have not come across any danger. I think some people have been exaggerating. The people who say the wolf is fierce, for example. When I met him he was perfectly courteous!"

"You have met the wolf?" asked the hunter slowly in disbelief.

"Of course! He told me where to find these flowers," Little Red Riding Hood replied simply, confusing the hunter even further.

"Take me to the spot where you met him so that I can follow his tracks."

"Okay, but we need to go quickly because I want to get to my grandmother's house in time for dinner," she said.

The hunter followed her and crossed the ravine with his eyes closed, trembling. He wondered how such a little girl could walk through the forest without coming to any harm. When they finally reached the clearing where Little Red Riding Hood had met the big, bad wolf, they parted.

The hunter had seen the footprints of the wolf on the path and began to follow them carefully. He told the child to take a different path, a shortcut that would take her to her grandmother's house safely.

Following the hunter's directions, Little Red Riding Hood finally reached her grandmother's cottage.

"Let's hope that Grandmother is ready for dinner, because I am very hungry," she said, knocking on the door.

Inside the house, the wolf heard the knocking and jumped back into bed. That little brat had finally found the way! Now it was time to carry out his plan. Trying to imitate the grandmother's voice, he called out: "Who is it?"

"It's Little Red Riding Hood, Grandmother. I'm here to keep you company."

"What a nice surprise, dear. Come inside and greet your grandmother!"

Little Red Riding Hood pushed open the door and went in. First, she went to the kitchen to set the basket on the table and prepare a tasty snack.

"Where are you, little one?" asked the wolf impatiently.

"I'm coming, Grandmother! You know, your voice sounds very strange."

"My voice is strange, you say? It's because . . . I have a sore throat," replied the wolf.

"Where can I find a vase?" asked Little Red Riding Hood as she entered her grandmother's room.

"A vase?" cried the wolf. "What do you want with a vase?"

"Oh, Grandmother, it's a wonderful tale. I met a very nice wolf."

"Nice?" asked the wolf. "Don't you mean fierce?"

"Not at all! That's what everyone believes, but he was actually very nice. He showed me where to find these colorful flowers. I went in search of them because I wanted to bring them to cheer up the house a little. And what do you know, they were right where he told me!"

"Really?" the wolf asked incredulously. He had invented the directions so that he would have time to get to the cottage before Little Red Riding Hood. But then she had actually found the wretched flowers!

"I also brought a delicious cake, and—"

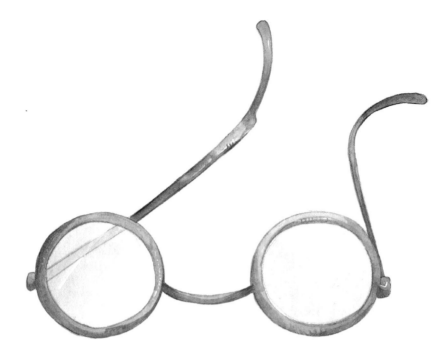

"Enough chattering, little one!" the wolf protested in exasperation. "Come closer to me."

Little Red Riding Hood moved closer while the wolf began to grind his teeth. "Grandmother, it's so dark in here. I'll open the curtains to let in a little sun so we can see better."

"No, Little Red Riding Hood, we don't need it," the wolf tried to explain, but a ray of sunshine had already illuminated his face.

"But Grandmother, what big ears you have!"

"All the better to hear you with."

"And your eyes . . . what big eyes you have today!"

"All the better to see you with."

"But . . . Grandmother, what a big mouth you have!"

"All the better to eat you with!" cried the wolf, jumping on the girl.

In an instant, there was no longer any trace of Little Red Riding Hood.

The wolf swallowed her in one gulp, as he had done with her grandmother. Happy and satisfied, he thought that his plan had turned out perfectly in the end!

Proudly, he imagined how every animal in the forest would be talking about it. They would admire the imagination and incredible ferocity of the most cunning hunter in the forest.

With these pleasant thoughts, he returned to the bed and fell asleep. He would have slept until the next day if an insistent noise had not woken him up. There was someone knocking at the door.

"Who is it?" he asked in a shrill voice.

"Good evening, ma'am. It's the hunter. I have seen wolf prints in the clearing. Have you seen him pass by?"

The hunter! The wolf hid under the covers and cried, "Go away!"

"I know that I have already disturbed you in the past, but if you could let me in for just a moment . . ."

The hunter noticed that the door was ajar, so he pushed it open and went inside.

The hunter had taken only a few steps into the cottage when something attacked him!

The big, bad wolf had been hiding behind the door when the hunter entered. He was determined to take care of the pesky man once and for all! Unfortunately, it was not the perfect day to take on this enemy. With the child and her grandmother in his belly, he felt very heavy. But he still caught the hunter by surprise.

In the moments that followed, the enemies fought fiercely. The hunter pulled out his knife and was about to stab the wolf when the animal bit him on the arm. He dropped the weapon on the ground. But the wolf stumbled and slammed against the wall with a yelp. The hunter did not let the opportunity escape. Picking up the knife, he lunged at the big, bad wolf and killed him with one swift movement. Panting, he watched the animal for a few minutes, until he realized that his belly was rising and falling.

"How is that possible?" the hunter wondered.

Then he looked around and saw that the house was empty.

"Where's the old lady? And her granddaughter?" he asked himself. Then a thought crept into his mind. Maybe the wolf had eaten them! But if they were still moving, did that mean that they were still alive? "I might still have time to save those poor people!"

The hunter grabbed his knife and made a small hole in the wolf's belly. Suddenly, out jumped Little Red Riding Hood and her grandmother!

They were frightened and battered, but safe and sound! Little Red Riding Hood and her grandmother embraced each other, and then they turned to the hunter.

"I had lost hope of anyone saving us!" exclaimed the grandmother.

"It was fortunate that I was passing and that I found the wolf's footprints in time," the hunter replied, smiling.

"Oh, thank you, thank you, Mr. Hunter!" said the little girl, hopping up and down. "Where would we be without you?"

"I've been hunting that wolf for a long time. So today is a special day for me, too. I can finally go home."

With that, the hunter heaved the body of the wolf onto his shoulders. He said good-bye to Little Red Riding Hood and her grandmother, then walked slowly toward home.

"Grandmother, I was very frightened!"

"Me, too, little one. Come here and tell me everything that has happened to you, right from the beginning. And then promise me that you will never disobey your mother again."

"I promise, Grandmother!"

And the little girl repeated the same promise to her mother, when finally she held her in her arms once more.

STERLING CHILDREN'S BOOKS
New York

An Imprint of Sterling Publishing
387 Park Avenue South
New York, NY 10016

First Sterling edition 2015
First published in Italy in 2014 by De Agostini Libri S.p.A.

© 2014 De Agostini Libri S.p.A.

ISBN 978-1-4549-1510-2

Distributed in Canada by Sterling Publishing
c/o Canadian Manda Group, 165 Dufferin Street
Toronto, Ontario, Canada M6K 3H6
For information about custom editions, special sales, and premium and corporate purchases,
please contact Sterling Special Sales at 800-805-5489 or specialsales@sterlingpublishing.com.

Translation: Contextus s.r.l., Pavia, Italy (Louise Bostock)
Editor: Contextus s.r.l., Pavia, Italy (Martin Maguire)

Manufactured in China
Lot #:
2 4 6 8 10 9 7 5 3 1
11/14
www.sterlingpublishing.com/kids